For Eloise, with love

By the same author

Miranda the Castaway

First published in Great Britain in 1997
by Orion Children's Books
a division of the Orion Publishing Group Ltd
Orion House
5 Upper St Martin's Lane
London WC2H 9EA

A catalogue record for this book is available
from the British Library

Designed by Dalia Hartman
Printed in Italy
ISBN 1 85881 176 7

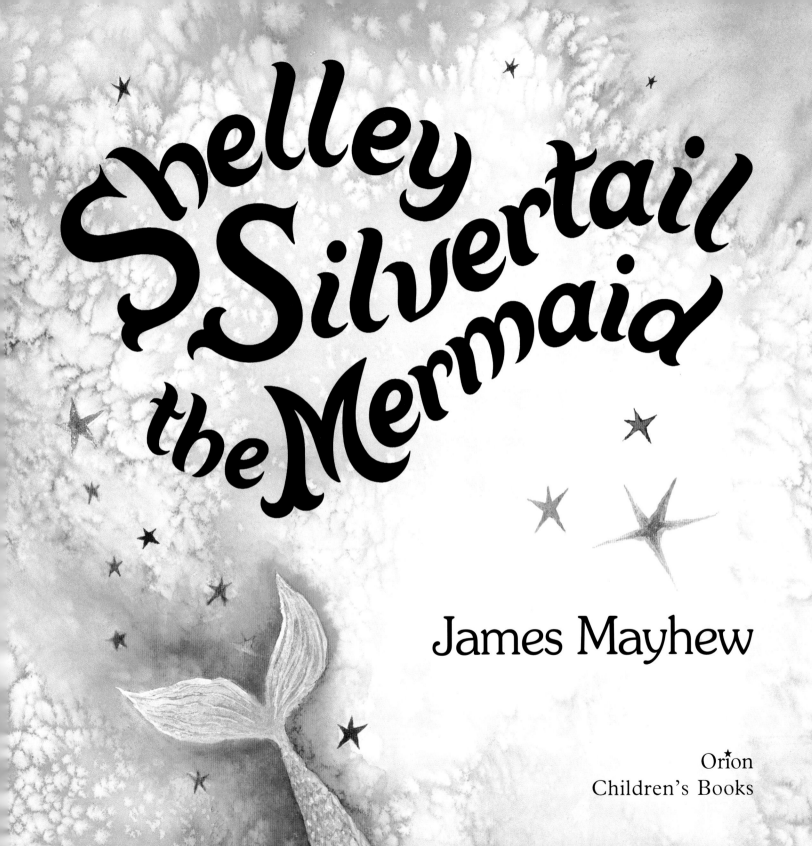

Shelley Silvertail the Mermaid

James Mayhew

Orion
Children's Books

Shelley Silvertail the mermaid sat under the moon combing
her golden hair.

A small grey seal bobbed up out of the water.

"Sing to me," said the seal.

"But I don't know how," said Shelley Silvertail.

"I thought all mermaids could sing," said the seal. "A mermaid who can't sing is like a fish who can't swim."

Shelley opened her mouth to try, but no song came out, just a sigh.

"If the other mermaids knew, they would all laugh at me!" said Shelley, diving into a wave.

"Please don't go," called the seal.

"I must find someone who can show me how to sing," said Shelley. "Then I'll come back."

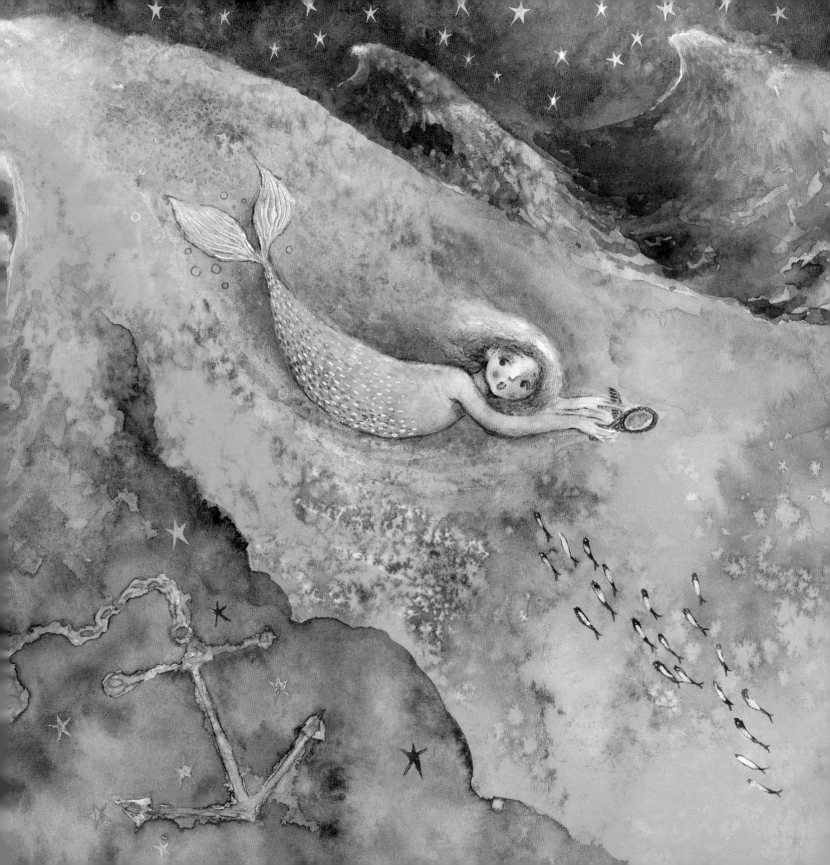

Shelley Silvertail swam and swam until she reached the warm tropical seas. Starfish, flying fish and angelfish filled the water with colour, while swordfish, turtles and seahorses played in the forests of seaweed.

"Can you show me how to sing, please?" she asked.

"We can't sing," said the swordfish.

"We can only fly," said the flying fish.

"Fish swim and mermaids sing," said the angelfish.

But Shelley couldn't sing, so she swam off over the coral reef and across the sea.

Shelley followed the current until she came to the turquoise waters of the Mediterranean.

She swam in and out of sunken cities with the squid and the tuna fish and the crabs.

"Who can show me how to sing?" said Shelley Silvertail.

"Not us," said the squid, squirting their ink at Shelley.

"Nor us," said the crabs, snapping their claws.

"We don't sing, we swim," said the tuna fish, blowing bubbles.

Shelley Silvertail swam the seven seas. When she reached the cold Antarctic she swam through the shipwrecks with narwhals, dolphins and penguins.

"Please," said Shelley Silvertail, "can anyone teach me how to sing?"

The dolphins played around her, the narwhals snorted, the penguins clapped their flippers.

"The great whales can sing," they said. "Perhaps they will show you how."

Shelley Silvertail waited. She heard a song echoing off the icebergs, and saw the great whales swimming towards her. They sang a deep booming song. It was very beautiful, but it was not the song of a mermaid.

Shelley swam away, back to the grey seal.

"I still don't know how to sing," said Shelley.

"Don't cry," said the grey seal. "I'm glad you came back. I missed you."

"It's good to be home," said Shelley.

One day a fleet of ships came with nets to catch fish. The dolphins and tuna fish lay silent, and the crabs and squid hid themselves away in dark caves.

But the little grey seal swam into the nets and couldn't get out.

Shelley knew she had to save her friend. If only someone could come to help her break the nets and set the seal free!

She called out, but her voice was too soft, just a sigh. She tried again, and this time her voice sounded stronger. Shelley could sing! And her voice poured out like silver, to match her tail.

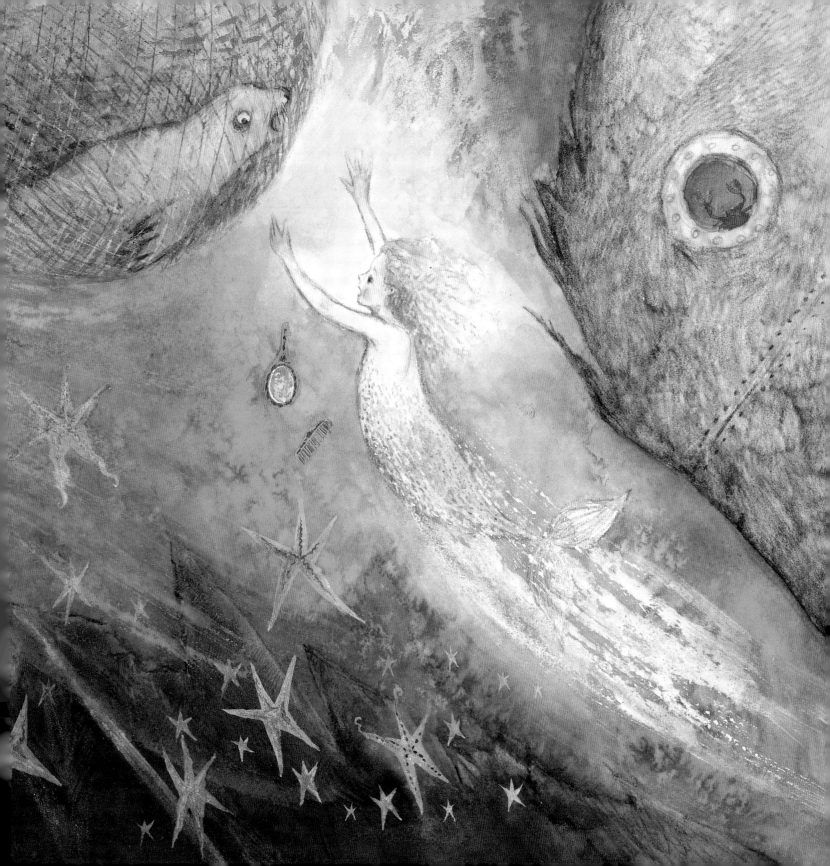

Shelley was afraid that the fishermen would hear and catch her too, but she kept on singing.

The fishermen didn't hear her. Perhaps their engines were too loud. Perhaps they didn't believe in mermaids.

The dolphins heard, and the tuna fish and the squid and the whales and turtles heard too. They came to break the nets, but the ropes were too strong.

Shelley sang on until her voice filled the seven seas.

Suddenly the sea was full of silver. Mermaids, mermen and merchildren swam towards the nets. They too had heard Shelley and they worked away at the knots with their fingers until, piece by piece, the nets fell apart and the seal was free.

"I can sing!" said Shelley, hugging the seal.

"I knew you could," said the seal. "All mermaids can sing."

"You sang beautifully!" said the other mermaids.

"Did I really?" said Shelley. "Then I'll sing all the time."

That night the mermaids came to listen to Shelley Silvertail singing. And Shelley sat under the moon combing her golden hair, while her voice, just a sigh at first, grew louder and louder until it poured from her mouth like silver, to match her tail.

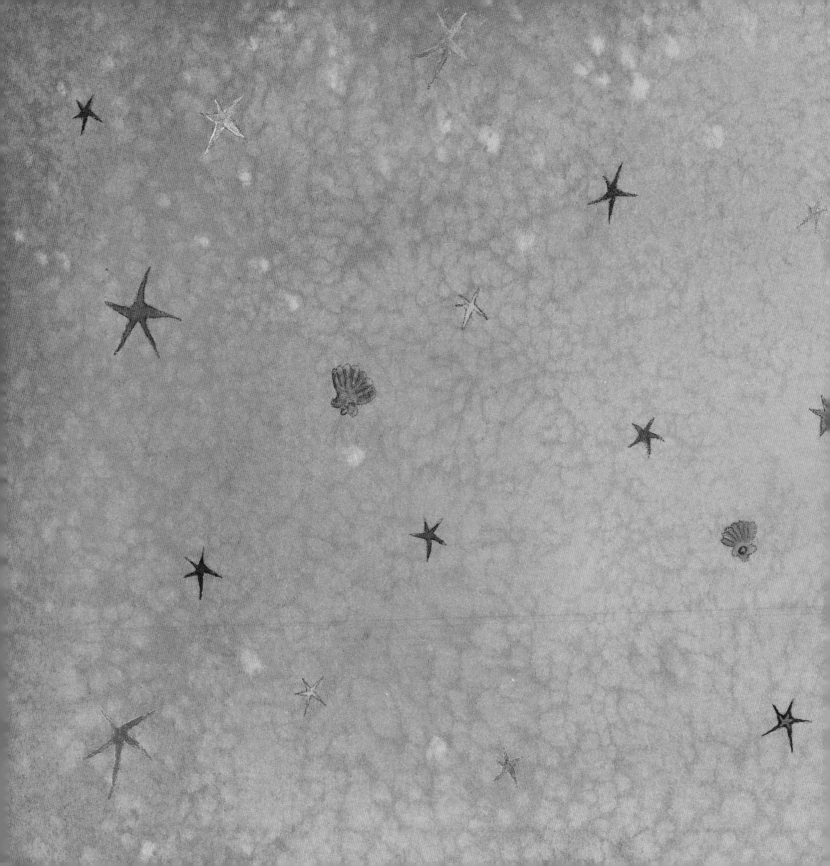